'It was probably due to the stran... s of their surroundings, but that night all three of them had dreams. Jinny dreamed of a black tower, black as soot. Robbie dreamed about cats. This was not surprising perhaps, considering what he had to put up with from Ginger, but these were real cats, lots of them. The strange thing was, although neither of them could possibly know it, both Robbie and Ginger were dreaming about the same cats. Ginger awoke suddenly. In the distance, she could hear a dog baying. For some reason her fur rose, and she began to hiss. Then she heard the answering call of cats.

"Those are real cats," she thought. "Real cats."

She had a feeling that, one day, she would meet a real cat and it would be important in some way. She felt calmer but uneasy. Was something going to happen?'

Katy's toys enjoy their peaceful life in the beautiful new cupboard-house. But then, one terrible night, Jinny the guinea pig is left outside and carried off by a savage dog. It seems that only the local cats can help now. But will they agree to join the toys in a desperate, dangerous rescue bid?

TROUBLE IN
THE CUPBOARD

TROUBLE IN THE CUPBOARD

Pat Thomson

Illustrated by Helen Cooper

YEARLING BOOKS

TROUBLE IN THE CUPBOARD

A YEARLING BOOK 0 440 862108

Originally published in Great Britain in 1987 by Victor
Gollancz Ltd

PRINTING HISTORY
Gollancz edition published 1987
Yearling edition published 1989

This book is set in 14/16 pt Century Textbook
by Colset Private Limited, Singapore.

Yearling Books are published by Transworld Publishers Ltd.,
61–63 Uxbridge Road, Ealing, London W5 5SA, in Australia by
Transworld Publishers (Australia) Pty. Ltd., 15–23 Helles
Avenue, Moorebank, NSW 2170, and in New Zealand by
Transworld Publishers (N.Z.) Ltd., Cnr. Moselle and Waipareira
Avenues, Henderson, Auckland.

Made and printed in Great Britain by
The Guernsey Press Co. Ltd, Guernsey,
Channel Islands

Contents

CHAPTER ONE

The House in the Cupboard

When Katy's dad came downstairs on Saturday morning, it was bad luck that Bear happened to be lying at the foot of the stairs. Dad trod on him, turned his ankle, and fell over the back of the armchair.

'Dratted toys,' he yelled. 'If Katy doesn't do something about all this junk, I'll lose my temper.'

'Steady on,' said Katy's mother, coming into the hall. 'What's all the fuss?'

'Fuss!' said Katy's dad indignantly. 'How would you like it if you had to go to work with your leg in a sling and explain that you did it by treading on a bear?'

'I promise you,' said Katy's mum, 'that you will never have to go to work with your leg in a sling. And anyway, you've been promising her a real toy cupboard for months. You said you would put a new door on the old hall cupboard.'

By the time Katy came down, Dad was feeling better and he was measuring in the hall. There was a deep cupboard in an alcove on one wall, but its hinges had been broken for a long time. Dad had said ages ago that, when he mended it, Katy could have it for a toy cupboard.

'Look, Katy,' said Dad. 'This cupboard is pointed at the top. It looks rather like a house.'

'Can it be a house?' asked Katy. 'Can you make the door like a front door?'

Dad looked at it and began to get quite keen on the idea.

'Don't see why not. In fact, I think I can do better than that.' He did a little drawing. He drew the side of a house with five windows and a little door.

'I can put the whole side of the house on hinges. That's the real cupboard door – but you can have a little front door as well. If I cut windows, you can have curtains or whatever you want. Perhaps you'd like a doorknocker?'

By the time he had finished, the cupboard looked just like a house. There were five rooms, all with a window, three of them upstairs and

two downstairs. There were painted window boxes and a smart front door. A brass handle from an old broken drawer made a very good knocker.

'That's it,' said Dad, pleased with himself. 'Now, perhaps we can have the floor back and walk in safety for a change.'

'Oh no, Dad,' said Katy. 'It's not an ordinary cupboard, it's a house. Only special people can live there. I'll have to think about it.'

Katy was saved from an argument by the doorbell. Their friendly postman handed over a package and was invited in to see the new cupboard house. You would have thought that Dad was going to live in it himself from the way he was talking. The postman declared himself very impressed.

'From what I've seen of all your toys, though, Katy,' he added, 'they'll be a bit overcrowded in there.'

He turned to go but hesitated on the doorstep.

'You don't have a real dog, do you?' he asked.

'No,' replied Dad. 'Why?'

'Had a bit of trouble along this road,' explained the postman. 'A dog went for me. Looked like a stray to me, really, but it was vicious. Nasty brute. Anyway,' he smiled again, 'just be a bit careful, Katy. It may still be hanging around. Good luck with the house.'

That night, inside the house, three animals sat round the table, feeling strange and not quite comfortable.

'Well, my old mates,' said a large ginger cat, 'this is a bit of a turn up, isn't it? First time I've had a room to myself. I usually sleep on Bear's head.'

'You would,' said Jinny. She was a fat little guinea-pig with a loud squeak. She had been a Christmas present when Katy was little, and her squeak used to make Katy laugh. Her greatest friend was the third animal, a black-and-white spotted dog called Robbie. Robbie was Katy's oldest toy. He was in all the old photographs of her in her pram. He was always calm and kind, and looked after the smaller toys. Bear was old, too. Granny had given Bear to Katy a long time ago. In fact, Katy could not remember a time when those three had not been around. Ginger, however, was a bit different. Dad's younger brother had bought her at the Youth Club jumble sale, and she had caused quite a stir when she arrived. Sometimes her fur was sleek and at other times it was ruffled, but there was always a wild look in her strange amber eyes. At least life had not been dull since Ginger's arrival. Things tended to happen. These days Katy did not play with the toys so much because she was at school, but they did not mind. It meant they could get on with their own lives, and now they even had a house of their own.

'I suppose we ought to get organized,' said Robbie. 'Shall we each have a room upstairs? Then this room can be the kitchen, as we have a nice table.'

'OK by me, Spotto,' said Ginger. 'I'll probably learn to play the drums in my room and keep black beetles.'

'You can't do that!' squeaked Jinny, getting excited. 'That would be terrible. What if they all escaped?'

'What? The drums?' asked Ginger. 'OK, OK,' she added quickly, as Jinny began to twitter crossly, 'keep your tail on. Who's going to have the other room?'

Jinny calmed down again, although she did not like the reference to her tail.

'I don't know. I suppose we could have visitors.'

'Owl or Mouse might like to come,' suggested Robbie. Owl was an old friend and often chatted to Robbie. He would enjoy visits from him. Mouse was small and tended to be nervous. Katy had made him herself out of scraps of material. He was a good sport, though, thought Robbie.

'Bear will come if there is any food,' said Ginger. 'You can rely on that guy to gobble up anything going.'

'You are very rude, Ginger,' said Jinny.

'Me?' said Ginger. 'Me? When I was last at Buckingham Palace, everyone thought I was a duchess.'

'If you're a duchess, I'm a Dutchman,' said Robbie, grinning.

'I'm definitely a duchess, as sure as your name is Robbie Van Tulip.'

'But it isn't,' said Jinny, looking puzzled.

Robbie burst out laughing. 'Never mind, Jinny,' he said. 'All I ask is that Mrs Henrietta James should only be invited for short periods. I can't stand too much of her.'

Mrs Henrietta James was a hen. She was kind-hearted, but she did fuss.

'If she comes,' growled Ginger,

'I'll pour boiling oil over her from upstairs.'

But Jinny was thinking about the house again.

'I know where there's some furniture and things,' she said, looking cheerful. 'We must arrange everything tomorrow. I do think I'm going to like this house.'

'Yes,' agreed Robbie. 'Tomorrow we'll make some plans.'

It was probably due to the strangeness of their surroundings, but that night all three of them had dreams. Jinny dreamed of a black tower, black as soot. Robbie dreamed about cats. This was not surprising perhaps, considering what he had to put up with from Ginger, but these were real cats, lots of them. The strange thing was, although neither of them could possibly know it, both Robbie and Ginger were dreaming about the same cats. Ginger awoke suddenly. In the distance, she could hear a dog baying.

For some reason her fur rose, and she began to hiss. Then she heard the answering call of cats.

'Those are real cats,' she thought. 'Real cats.'

She had a feeling that, one day, she would meet a real cat and it would be important in some way. She felt calmer but uneasy. Was something going to happen?

'Oh, rubbish!' she said to herself. 'I must get a good night's sleep so that I can be really lively tomorrow. This place would be rock-bottom boring without me.'

And pushing all uncomfortable thoughts away, she wrapped her tail snugly round her nose and fell fast asleep.

CHAPTER TWO

Birthday Ghost

'Good morning, Robbie,' said Jinny. 'I'm just getting breakfast ready. Come and have some.'

Robbie came into the kitchen, where Jinny was getting herself organized and feeling very much at home.

'I like this house,' said Robbie. 'Katy has made us very comfortable. We could do all sorts of things here, you know.'

The house was somehow quite different when the door was closed. It did not seem like a cupboard at all.

'Katy made me a special bed,' said Jinny happily, 'with a matching cover and pillowcase.'

'Hello, you guys,' said a voice from the kitchen door. 'Is there any food in this dump?'

Robbie started to laugh, but Jinny looked a bit cross.

'Come in, Ginger,' she said. 'There is some food and this is *not* a dump.'

'OK. Keep your tail on,' said Ginger, sliding into the kitchen and leaping noiselessly into a chair. 'This is delicious, kid. Are you going to be our cook?'

'Well,' said Robbie, 'I think we should be fair about this. If Jinny does the cooking, we should do other jobs. I could do the housework. What about you, Ginger?'

'I'll keep down the mice.'

'Oh, wonderful!' said Jinny. 'There's only one mouse and he's my friend.'

'You see?' said Ginger. 'I'm really good at my job. I've got the mice down to one already. I could also look after the milk.'

'Yes, thank you, Ginger,' broke in

Robbie hastily. 'I don't think that's the best job for you. We'll think of something later.'

'If you're so good at everything, Ginger,' said Jinny crossly, 'you could protect us. I heard Katy talking about something horrid this morning.'

Then Jinny stopped looking cross and started looking anxious.

'Don't worry, Jinny,' Robbie said kindly. 'It's only a stray dog. You know Katy is rather nervous about real dogs.'

'It sounds more dangerous than that,' Jinny answered. She was serious now. 'A horrible dog has been roaming the countryside around here, and there's even talk about someone's pet being hurt.' She swallowed hard.

'Oh, great!' said Ginger. 'A huge ravenous beast is beating up all the small creatures round here, and you want me to sort it out. That's Robbie's job. There's no such thing as a guard cat. When I join the Police

Cats, I'll let you know.'

'Look here, said Robbie, 'these are nothing but stories. We don't really know if they are true. And anyway, what harm can come to us in here? Let's change the subject. Just now, I think we ought to arrange a party, a house-warming, and invite all the toys to it.'

Jinny cheered up at once. 'That's a good idea. It's Bear's birthday soon, so it could be his party, too. I was going to make him a cake, anyway.' She got quite excited. 'Let's write the invitations, and we must have games. And what about prizes? We must have prizes.'

'If there's going to be a party, kids, you can rely on me to make it swing,' said Ginger. She lashed her tail twice, and then settled down very thoughtfully and began to purr.

The toys were very pleased to be invited to the new house, and arrived early. Bear was thrilled to be the special guest.

'I like your house, Jinny,' he said, 'and the cake. I like your smart room, and the sandwiches. I like your kitchen, too, and the sticky buns.'

'Is your name Tum-Tum?' asked Ginger.

'No,' said Bear, puzzled. 'It's Bear.'

'Don't take any notice of her,' said Jinny quickly. 'Look, we've got you a bag of sweets for your birthday present. Here comes little Owl. Come in, Owl.'

A little white owl hopped over the step. He was soft and fluffy, and Jinny thought he was really sweet. She sometimes made him be the baby when she and Katy played with the dolls' pram, even though his claws kept catching in the shawl. The strange thing was, he wasn't a bit afraid of Ginger. He just smiled at her and murmured, 'Hiya, Pussycat,' and Ginger smiled too, and looked out of the window. Just then there was a terrible flurry and fuss, and a great squawking at the door.

'Watch it, guys,' called Ginger. 'The horrendous Henrietta is here. Old fusspot is with us.'

Mrs Henrietta James was rather a fussy hen. The others just thought she was a show-off and a nuisance, but Henrietta did not see it like that. She knew she was a very important person, a leader in society and worthy of special interest. She had this idea because if you pressed her back down she laid an egg. In fact, Katy had lost the wooden egg a long time ago and now Mrs Henrietta laid a ping-pong ball, but that did not affect her self-importance.

'My dears,' she would say, 'I am not like you. I have special gifts.'

Robbie felt rather sorry for her and invited her in kindly.

'I've walked so far, my dear,' she said, 'I must have a teensy-weensy rest, or I shall die. I shall truly die.'

'Go on, then,' said Ginger in an interested voice. 'Can we watch?'

'Round the table, everyone,' said Robbie. 'You come to the top, Bear; it's your birthday. You sit here, Mrs Henrietta, between Jinny and me. Ginger, you and Owl can sit at the other end. Ah, Mouse, you've come at last. You're just in time. Come and sit down.'

'Yes, come on Mouse,' said Ginger. 'Sit between Owl and my good self. We'll look after you.'

'Don't be such a tease,' said Jinny. 'He'll sit next to me.'

'All right. Keep your tail on. Let's get those candles lit before Bear eats them.'

The party began with them all singing 'Happy Birthday'. Mrs Henrietta said that in the best families it was sung at the *end* of a party; but Robbie said there were no rules really, so they sang it several times, whenever they felt like it. Katy had saved all sorts of things out of the Christmas crackers, so Jinny wrapped them all up again and they

each had a little present. Everyone
laughed and talked, and passed
around the plates. Ginger even
went to and fro pouring out the
orange juice. When she came to
Mrs Henrietta she leaned rather
heavily on her, and then gave a cry
of surprise:

'Mrs Henrietta! You've laid a
doughnut!'

Poor Mrs Henrietta leaped up with
a strangled squawk.

'You're right,' she clucked nervously. 'Oh my dears, my special gifts! They've gone all sugary. What shall I do?'

'Now, Ginger,' said Robbie. 'I did see that you had a doughnut in your paw just before you reached Mrs Henrietta. Could you have dropped it?'

'Good gracious!' said Ginger. 'I believe you're right. False alarm, Mrs H.'

Mrs Henrietta looked hard at Ginger.

'Fiend! Villain! Hearth Rug!' she hissed. 'You did it on purpose.'

'Perhaps we ought to have a few games now,' said Ginger mildly. Robbie was good at organizing games and was very clever at awarding the prizes so that no one was disappointed. They were saving the best game until last.

'What about Sardines?' said Robbie.

'Great,' said Ginger. 'I feel a bit hungry.'

'No, the game,' Robbie explained. 'We turn the lights out, one of us goes to hide, and then we all try to find that person. If you do, keep very quiet and hide with them, until we are all squashed together like sardines! Owl had better be the one to hide first as he can see in the dark anyway.'

The lights were turned off, Owl fluttered quietly away, and the others began to count to one hundred.

'Coming!' they all shouted, and scrambled out of the room. Suddenly, the house became very quiet in the dark. Even Mrs Henrietta was silent. Jinny wished she had stayed near Robbie, but she crept quietly upstairs. She looked under the beds first but found no one. She looked in the wardrobe but there was no sign of Owl. She slipped out to the landing again and saw Mouse coming upstairs. Then she noticed the airing cupboard door. It was slightly open. She was sure it had been closed before the party began. Before Mouse could see, she slid into the cupboard.

'Are you there, Owl?' she whispered.

There was a slight movement. Jinny smiled to herself and curled up in the bottom of the cupboard. The next moment, Mouse slipped in beside her.

'Who's here?' he asked.

Jinny did not answer but giggled, and they could both hear the sound of breathing above them. After several minutes, Mrs Henrietta found them. She pecked inside the cupboard and Mouse couldn't help saying 'Ow', but he did it very quietly. She took a little time to settle down and insisted on fluffing out her feathers so much that Robbie heard her. It was becoming quite a squash now and they laughed a little, but rather quietly and nervously. They could just see a faintly moving white shape above them. Jinny suddenly thought that the shape did not sound like Owl. It was hissing slightly in a rather frightening way. Just then, a voice came from downstairs.

'Where are you all?' It was Owl's voice. 'No one has found me yet. What's happening?'

The hissing noise grew louder and the white shape reared up, growing to three times the size of Owl, then growling ferociously. With great shrieks, the toys threw themselves out of the cupboard. The door banged back. Mrs Henrietta shouted, 'A ghost! A ghost!' Jinny shouted, 'Help, Help!' Mouse shouted, 'Ow! Ow!' because Robbie trod on him. Poor Owl stood halfway up the stairs looking amazed.

'But what *are* you doing?' he asked.

No one could answer. They surged across the landing, tripping and clutching at each other. Owl had to flap his wings to keep his balance, then, infected by the panic, ran with them. The white shape came on, relentlessly pursuing. They rushed in one direction, then turned like a flock of agitated birds and wheeled round.

The white shape followed. Into the kitchen they poured and took refuge under the table.

'Get behind me, everyone,' said Robbie, and he pulled the tablecloth down on one side to hide them. The half-finished trifle crashed to the floor.

Smash! That was the glass bowl.

Splat! That was the trifle.

'Ooh!' Was that the ghostly creature?

Robbie looked out from under the cloth. The strange white shape was still there but it did not quite reach the ground. It was not floating, either. In the gap between the whiteness and the floor, there were, quite definitely four ginger paws. Robbie said sternly,

'Ginger, take that pillowcase off at once.'

'Hi, you guys,' said Ginger. 'Good game. Very exciting, I thought.'

The others peeped out from under the table.

'Why are you wearing that cloth on your heads?' asked Ginger. 'Playing at weddings, are we?'

Robbie started to laugh.

'I'm a bit warm,' he said. 'Let's all have some orange juice and see about some going-home presents. We'll take a vote on whether ghosts get a present, so, Ginger, you'd better start being nice to us now!'

And puffing and panting, and very much relieved, they all tumbled out from under the table. They felt they ought to be cross with Ginger, but it had been rather an exciting birthday party.

CHAPTER THREE

Visitors from Down Under

Katy's house was so noisy these days that Robbie and Jinny hardly heard the knock on the cupboard house door. Mouse came in, looking puzzled.

'There's some howling luggage in the hall,' he said.

Jinny opened her eyes wide.

'Howling luggage?' she said. 'Let's look.'

They went to the window and, sure enough, there was a big blue bag with handles, and loud noises were coming from it. Ginger came up behind them and stared too.

'That's a carrycot,' said Robbie. 'Katy used to have one. It must be a baby making all that noise, but what's it doing here?'

'This is a job for the Secret Service,' said Ginger. 'Agent 123 will go on a mission and will not return until she has the information.' And with that, she slipped out of the door.

She did not come back until nearly an hour later, looking rather ruffled and strangely damp.

'It was terrible,' she reported. 'I could never be a real agent. I can't stand such suffering.'

'What on earth happened?' asked Jinny, all concern.

'I was just looking at the baby thing, searching for clues, when someone came up behind me and said – this is absolutely true – this woman said, "Did oo throw the ickle pussy out, then?" And what happens next? She picks me up and puts me in the carrycot!'

'Oh help!' said Jinny sympathetically.

'First I was nearly deafened; then it

gets hold of me and puts my tail in its mouth.'

'How disgusting,' said Robbie. 'It's because they're teething, you know.'

'Huh!' said Ginger. 'Good thing it had no teeth, or I'd be a Manx cat. Anyway, I was brave. I didn't flinch. I listened with both ears and found out what's happening.'

'Great,' said Robbie. 'What's going on?'

'The new people are Katy's cousins and their parents. Granny is staying too, because the cousins have come all the way from Australia. It's a special visit.'

'Yes, it's ever such a long way,' nodded Jinny. 'It must be the first time they've seen the cousins.'

'But that's not all,' continued Ginger. 'Having ruined the curl in my tail, this baby thing threw me out, and the woman picked me up and put me on the armchair – and I've met someone!'

Jinny and Robbie were very

interested.

'More Australians?'

'Yes. A Kangaroo, and one I'm not sure about – it looks like a little bear, but I don't think it can be a proper bear. Anyway, they're very friendly and I've arranged a meeting for tonight.'

'Well done, Agent 123,' said Robbie. 'Go and dry your tail, and we'll tell the others.'

That night, they all gathered in the cupboard house and waited. As soon as the family settled down, they trooped out and approached the armchair.

'Good-day,' said the Kangaroo. 'We're very pleased to meet you. Ginger told us all about you. I'm Kangaroo, and this is my friend Wombat.'

'It doesn't look like a bat,' said Owl.

'No, no,' said Kangaroo. 'She's not a bat.'

The wombat smiled sleepily, then

started to snore.

'You'll have to excuse her,' explained Kangaroo. 'She's jet-lagged.'

'She's what-lagged?' asked Ginger. 'You'll have to tell us about your-selves. We only go as far as the corner shop.'

'Well,' said Kangaroo. 'We've come a very long way in an aeroplane. Australia is on the other side of the world. In fact, we're just going to sleep when you're getting up. So, you see, when you fly from Australia, you're likely to be offered breakfast just as it's really suppertime, and all you want to do is go to bed.'

Bear looked interested.

'Do you mean,' he said, 'that if I had breakfast here and then went to Australia, I could get two breakfasts the same day?'

Kangaroo grinned. 'You could probably manage something like that.'

Bear began to think of becoming

an airline pilot. If he organized it properly, somewhere it was probably always dinnertime.

'Are there any more animals like you in Australia?' asked Mouse.

'Certainly,' said Kangaroo. 'We are rather special because we are marsupials; that is, animals with pouches. You know, with pockets for the young animals to live in.'

'How very *useful*, dears,' said Mrs Henrietta James admiringly. 'So convenient!'

'This is quite fascinating,' said Robbie. 'Do come into our house and tell us all about it. Make yourselves at home.'

They returned to the house, with Kangaroo hopping cheerfully and Wombat leaning sleepily on Robbie and Bear. Jinny got out the orange juice and biscuits. Kangaroo turned out to be an excellent storyteller. He told them about the long journey, how large and different Australia was, and described animals there, which are never found in this country. He told them about the duck-billed platypus, a furry animal with a duck-like beak which lays eggs.

'Well!' said Mouse. 'We don't have anything like that.'

'Thought I saw a dingo when I arrived,' said Kangaroo.

'What's a dingo?' asked Robbie. 'I don't think we have those.'

'Kind of dog,' explained Kangaroo. 'Dirty-yellow colour, mainly, and they can be nasty. There are even stories about them attacking children.'

'We don't have anything like that,' Jinny burst in quickly.

'Just wondered,' said Kangaroo. 'There was a bit of a fuss when we drove up. One of these things was trying to get under your gate and Katy's father had to take a stick and drive it off.'

The toys fell silent. It was very unpleasant. Every day someone mentioned the dog. There were even rumours of two dogs. One certainly did seem to be lurking in the street outside the garden. Sometimes Katy would climb up, look over the fence and scream. Their hearts would stop. Then Katy's mother would run out and tell her not to be so silly.

'It can't get into the garden,' she would say.

They explained to Kangaroo that Katy was nervous, and this made them all jumpy.

Ginger snorted. 'You can't tell a kangaroo you're jumpy,' she giggled.

They all started to laugh again, and it was lucky that Owl's sharp ears heard the family begin to stir. They realized it was getting light. They only just had time to haul Wombat back into the armchair. As they hurried back into the cupboard house, Ginger whispered to the others:

'I've had an idea. The next time the family all go out, let's have an Australian Day.'

Eventually the chance came. Everyone was to go on a special visit to London. Granny was going to stay at home and rest her feet, so she would look after the baby who was not interested in the Crown Jewels. The sun shone as the family got off to an early start. The toys waited until it was quiet and then sent Mouse off to investigate.

'Granny's sitting in the front garden, with the baby asleep beside her. She's got lots of books and the paper, and she's got her knitting, too.'

'Good,' said Ginger. 'Get everything ready. We'll go into the back garden.'

They started off by crossing the Great Australian Desert in the sandpit. Owl was rather a good actor. He staggered and groaned, and then threw himself at the paddling pool, croaking, 'Water, water!' Ginger had a box with her and kept bringing useful things out of it. She put a lampshade on Wombat's head because, as she explained, if Wombat fell asleep in the hot Australian sun, she might die of sunstroke. She had things for the paddling pool, too. She threw in large stones and the car-cleaning sponge.

'The Great Barrier Reef,' she announced. She also threw in some coloured beads. 'Now we have to go underwater fishing and catch these jewel-like fishes.'

They all leaned over the edge and tried to reach the beads.

Mouse could not manage. He kept jumping up and grabbing the sides of the pool, but every time he slipped back on to the grass. Then Robbie helped him on to the edge, but it was still too slippery and he got very nervous.

'I want to see! I want to see!' he insisted. Then, 'Ow, ow!' he squeaked.

Ginger had found a clothes peg and fastened his tail to the edge of the pool.

'Look,' said Robbie. 'Katy's plastic

boat is quite big. You would be quite safe and we could tie the string to the plug of the pool, just to make sure.'

Mouse was delighted, even more so when Kangaroo told him about the pirate treasure-hunters of the southern seas.

'Yo ho ho,' squeaked Mouse. 'Avast me hearties!' And Robbie kindly gave him a lolly stick for a sword.

'You must be careful, Mouse,' continued Kangaroo, 'because there is one danger in these warm waters. If you see a triangular fin cutting through the water, coming straight for you, it could be a shark. They bask offshore, and sometimes, when people are cheerfully swimming, they see a flurry of waves and bubbles, then—'

There was a splash and a churning of water, and Ginger's voice cried out, 'Shark, shark!' Coming across the pool at speed was a fish shape with gaping jaws. Owl and Kangaroo jumped backwards. Mrs Henrietta James was so confused, she jumped forward into the pool. Robbie pulled in Mouse's boat so fast, that Mouse shot off the back and found himself clinging to the sponge. Only Ginger was calm as the fish-shaped nailbrush, which she had just thrown into the pool, bobbed harmlessly against Wombat's paws. Wombat had fallen asleep again, holding on to the pool. Everyone had to be helped out, wrung out and calmed down.

'It was only Katy's nailbrush,' said Ginger innocently. 'How was I to know you would all go mad?'

'That cat will be the death of me,' sighed Mrs Henrietta.

'I think it's time for the barbecue,' said Jinny. 'We could all do with a peaceful half-hour.' She looked hard at Ginger. Ginger put a paper plate in her mouth.

'Mmm mmm mmm,' she said. She took the plate out and explained, 'I'm a duck-billed platypus.'

'You'll be a red-nosed flatty-puss if you try any more tricks like the last one,' Bear told her.

Kangaroo was the only one allowed to set up the barbecue, and he did it in the sandpit for safety. He told them how it was quite usual to eat out of doors in Australia, and he also taught them to sing 'Waltzing Matilda' when they had finished eating.

'This has been really nice,' said Robbie. 'I hope you will be able to visit us again one day.'

'Let's play hide-and-seek before we have to go in,' suggested Jinny. 'Not Sardines,' she added quickly, 'just hide-and-seek.'

Ginger stared up at the clouds.

'Would you like to play, Wombat?' asked Robbie.

'Certainly. Lovely idea,' she nodded, then nodded off completely, so they left her propped up against the sandpit. Looking at her, Mouse started to yawn. He was not sure if it was the shock and excitement of the shark, or whether Wombat's sleepiness was catching.

Jinny hid first. She found a good place in a flowerpot. Robbie was soon found when it was his turn. He hid in Ginger's cardboard box, but left his spotty tail hanging out.

'Who's next? Who's next?' they shouted.

'It must be Mouse,' said Ginger.

'No, it's my turn,' said Owl.

'Well, Mouse isn't here,' said Ginger, 'so he must be hiding already.'

'Oh, all right,' said Owl, good-naturedly. 'Off we go.'

They looked everywhere. They scoured the back garden.

'You're doing really well, Mouse,' called Jinny. 'We can't find you.'

They even crept round to the front garden, where Granny was chatting over the fence as she watched for the return of the family.

'He can't have gone that way,' said Robbie. 'Perhaps he went indoors.'

'I don't think so,' said Mrs Henrietta James. 'He would have passed me.'

'Mouse,' called Robbie. 'We give up. Come out.'

No answer.

'You've won, Mouse,' shouted Robbie, getting just a bit worried. 'Come out now.'

No answer.

'I think something must have happened,' said Jinny. 'He would come out if he could.'

'Perhaps he's trapped,' suggested Owl anxiously.

'He'd call out, I think,' said Robbie. 'Let's be very quiet.'

They remained absolutely still, only Ginger gently lashing her tail. There was no sound except the birds, distant shouts of children, and Wombat's gentle snores.

Wombat did sound a bit odd. It was a kind of double snore, a gentle regular snore, and a squeaky, muffled one. Robbie looked hard at Ginger.

'Ah, yes,' said Ginger. 'Well, you see, Mouse fell asleep and I didn't

want him to miss his turn, so I hid
him.'

They all looked at Wombat.

'In there?' whispered Jinny, sound-
ing very shocked.

Suddenly, Wombat's pocket wriggled a bit and Mouse's nose peeped
out.

'Where am I?' he asked, looking
round in surprise. 'Oh my goodness!'
He hopped out quickly.

'Really, Ginger!' said Jinny. 'You
are a disgrace. You are—' She could

not find a word bad enough. 'Outrageous!' she finished.

'You certainly are outrageous,' bristled Mrs Henrietta James. 'What does it mean? No, don't tell me. Ginger must be it, whatever it is.'

Ginger sat down and washed a paw.

'Just being helpful, old mates,' she murmured.

'I shouldn't worry,' said Kangaroo. 'Wombat hasn't even woken up.'

'We must get in quickly, anyway,' said Robbie. 'You see what we have to put up with, Kangaroo?'

They all heaved Wombat on to Robbie's back, and walked back to the house.

'It was rather a good Australian Day,' said Mouse, as they helped Wombat into the armchair; and when Ginger went upstairs to put the nail-brush back, they started to giggle.

But by the time the family burst in, the hall was quiet and the cupboard door was firmly closed, as if nothing had happened at all.

CHAPTER FOUR

A Very Important Person

Ginger was sitting up on the window-sill, as usual. Suddenly she stood up and hissed slightly.

'Don't look now, my treasures,' she said, 'but that awful cousin has come, and she's carrying Chocolate Tom.'

'Oh no!' Jinny rushed to the window. '*And* they've got a suitcase. That means an overnight stay.'

'Or even longer,' said Robbie, gloomily.

'No,' said Ginger. 'Katy's mum can't stand the awful cousin for more than one night. I've heard her say so. We can't stand Chocolate Tom for longer than that, either.'

'Maybe Katy won't open the cupboard house today,' suggested Jinny hopefully, but it didn't seem likely.

They watched the awful cousin. She was carrying a toy cat with beautiful chocolate-coloured markings on its cream fur. She had thrown everything else on the floor and seemed to be kicking the armchair. Katy was staring at her.

'I won't stay,' the cousin shouted. 'You can't make me. I want to come to the party with you.'

'It's only for one night, my darling,' replied the mother anxiously. 'Mummy wouldn't leave you for long, my pet, and I'll bring you lots of sweeties when I come back.'

'Oh yuck!' said Ginger. 'I'd bring her a packet of worms, and I'd bring that stuck-up Tom a bag of flea powder. I'd booby-trap their beds. I'd put syrup on their seats. I'd—'

'Yes, all right, Ginger,' interrupted Robbie. 'We all feel the same about them. It's just as Jinny says; let's lie low and hope no one remembers us.'

Unfortunately, they were not lucky. After tea, Katy tried to play cards and board games with her cousin, but she fussed if she lost and said the game was boring if she won. Katy got desperate and told her about the new house.

'It's a real house. Dad and I made it. The toys live in it, and they have their own rooms and a kitchen and everything. I sometimes feel that when I shut the door it becomes more real, somehow.'

'You must be stupid, then,' said the cousin. 'Show me anyway.'

Katy took her over to the little front door, and showed her the door knocker and the windows with their window-boxes.

'They're just painted,' sneered the cousin. 'Anyone can see it's just a cupboard. The whole front opens. Look.'

Robbie, Jinny and Ginger kept very still.

'These are my best toys,' said Katy

in a small voice. 'They have a room each.'

'What's that extra one for, then?' asked the cousin.

'It's a spare one. For visitors.'

'In that case, my Thomas Chocolate Paws can stay there. He'll be guest of honour. I'll go and get him,' she said, and slammed the door.

'Oh no!' said Robbie, as soon as they had gone.

'He'll want his supper,' said Jinny anxiously. 'I must go and cook something.'

'I'll cook something,' said Ginger. 'I'll cook Chokky Tom. I'll scratch his fur out.' She started to spit.

'I know he's awful,' sighed Robbie, 'but it's only for one night. It's no use getting worked up. We'll just have to make the best of it.'

'I will,' said Ginger thoughtfully. 'I think I know a way of making the best of it,' and she began to purr.

'Oh help!' said Robbie, and started to lay the table.

Thomas Chocolate Paws arrived just before supper. He was rather put-out.

'Why have I been put in this cupboard?' he demanded. Robbie had just been about to welcome him to the new house, so he did not say anything.

'I always sleep on my Mistress's bed. I am used to a silk cushion and absolutely no draughts. What shall I do?'

Robbie thought he sounded as if he was alone on a large stage and expected everyone to be looking at him. Jinny came hurrying through.

'Oh dear,' she said, looking rather hot and bothered. 'Supper's nearly ready. I do hope you like it.'

'Is this the cook?' asked Thomas, hardly looking at Jinny.

'Well, yes,' Robbie answered. 'This is Jinny. One of Katy's oldest toys. We all work together here, and Jinny does the cooking.'

'I see,' said Thomas. 'How very

strange. I hope I never have to work. How perfectly dreadful. It must ruin one's fur. But then, I am rather special. I have quite a pedigree, you know, and *that* makes one rather different from others.'

He turned to Jinny. 'Had you not better take your apron off? It looks rather common.'

Robbie was about to reply, when suddenly he saw that Ginger was standing in the doorway. She had been listening.

'Now for the fireworks,' thought Robbie, but nothing of the sort happened. Instead, Ginger bounced through the door crying, 'Thomas, darling! How super to see you!'

She had even brushed her fur and was wearing a large pink bow. Robbie could hardly believe his eyes.

'You must sit next to me, Thomas,' she purred. 'I'm dying to talk to you. You go to such exciting places and talk about such interesting things. It's a thrill to have you here!'

For the first time, Thomas smiled. This ginger cat was rather common, too, but at least she recognized that he was someone special. He allowed himself to be placed at the head of the table and fussed over. Ginger ran and fetched him a cushion. He did not need it, but accepted it graciously (though it meant that he was too high up and wobbled a bit).

Robbie and Jinny stared at them. They did not need to talk. Thomas began to tell them everything he had done and everything he thought, all of it boring. The only other voice was Ginger's, saying, 'How wonderful, Thomas,' or 'You are so right, Thomas.' Jinny and Robbie looked at each other. Robbie shrugged and twitched his nose, so Jinny began to serve supper. As the first course arrived, Ginger put her paw gently on Thomas's beautiful chocolate-and-cream one.

'Now, Thomas,' she said, 'we have our little ways here, too. We eat special food. We don't just think of our stomachs. For us, food has to *mean* something. Ordinary food is for ordinary people. Don't you agree?'

'Oh, er, quite. Yes,' replied Thomas, but he did not look entirely comfortable.

'This,' announced Ginger, as Jinny set the plate in front of Thomas, 'is the heart of a giant octopus.'

Robbie looked at his plate in amazement. It was a piece of nice fresh haddock. He looked at Ginger for an explanation, but she had closed her eyes and was saying:

'We hope to gain a little of the courage of the great creature. See, the heart has only just stopped beating.'

'Er . . . I never eat starters,' said Thomas faintly.

The others ate theirs at once. They liked haddock.

'Now, the second course. You will adore this,' Ginger assured Thomas. 'Just look. Freshly gathered earthworms, well scrubbed of course, topped by a finely minced mixture of acorns and death cap mushrooms. I spent hours this morning extracting the poison, so there's no danger. We like to be close to nature, you see. It refreshes us.'

'Quite so,' said Thomas, twiddling his fork.

Robbie started to eat heartily. It was minced beef with spaghetti, topped with perfectly ordinary mushrooms. They often had it. Jinny's eyes had grown very big listening to Ginger, but she was eating too. Ginger was delicately munching, uttering

little cries of 'Delicious!' and 'Delight-ful!' at intervals. Only Thomas did not seem to be enjoying it. His plate was almost full when it was cleared away. Robbie wondered what the pudding would be. It was supposed to be rice pudding with jam.

'Ah! Frogspawn with cockroach blood,' cried Ginger. 'We are not clever like you, Thomas, but we know about good things to eat! All our food is natural.'

Thomas got up quickly from his chair.

'Forgive me,' he said. His lovely cream fur looked oddly green. 'I'm rather tired after my journey. Perhaps I should go to bed.'

Ginger immediately jumped up.

'Poor Thomas! I'll show you to your room at once. This way.'

When Ginger came back into the kitchen, she was purring. She pulled off the pink ribbon, and began to pat it and nip it.

'No imagination, that cat,' she said.

'No sense of adventure either.'

'You were a bit hard on him,' said Robbie, finishing his pudding and licking the jam off his nose with a long tongue. (Jinny was eating Thomas's pudding as well as her own.)

'He said he liked new experiences. You heard him,' said Ginger. 'I was going to take him out and introduce him to that stray dog. That would have ruffled his fur a bit.'

Robbie shook his head. 'It's no use. You always make me laugh in the end.'

'I hope he feels all right,' said kind Jinny.

'Only a bit hungry,' replied Ginger, 'though he won't get much sleep tonight.'

'Whatever do you mean?' asked Jinny.

'I borrowed a couple of spare growls from Bear and put them under the mattress. Whenever he turns over, his bed will growl at him. Poor old Chokky Bits.'

The next morning, Jinny took Thomas a cup of tea.

'He says he isn't coming to breakfast,' she reported. 'He's rather tired. He says he'll stay in his room until it's time to go home.'

'How strange,' murmured Ginger. 'I thought he'd be keen to get to breakfast. I had a really good one worked out for him. Ah well, it won't stop us enjoying ours. Come on, chaps. Let's get stuck in. I'm starving.'

Jinny smiled as she put Ginger's plate in front of her.

'You deserve this, I have to admit it. It's all lovely and quiet again. Katy hasn't mentioned that awful dog once this week, so that must have gone as well. Everything is getting back to normal.'

Jinny was contented in the little cupboard house, but she was unfortunately quite wrong. Something was going to happen very soon.

CHAPTER FIVE

A Terrible Event

One day, Owl arrived with a very shocking story to tell. Katy had taken him out in the dolls' pram that morning. She sometimes took the toys out like that and, at the same time, she took next-door's puppy for a walk. Owl said they were walking along the pavement when they saw a big dog coming towards them. Katy tied the puppy's lead to the pram and crossed the road. The big dog stopped and stared at them. He was as tall as the pram, a yellow-brown colour, with rough hair and cruel teeth, which he showed as he looked across at them. His growl was long and menacing. Then, suddenly, he hurled himself across the road.

The puppy raced away, dragging the pram with Owl inside. Owl said it was terrifying, being thrown from side to side and up against the hood. Then the great dog leaped on the puppy, and the pram fell on its side. Owl was thrown out, fortunately still wrapped in the blankets. Katy, who had also been knocked down, screamed, and the lady from the newsagents, who knew them well, ran out and shouted. If it had not been for

an old man who bravely drove the dog off with his stick, Owl did not know what might have happened. The lady from the newsagents picked the pram up, put Owl back in it, and, carrying the frightened puppy, brought them all home. Katy was having her grazed knee bathed, and was still crying a bit. But that was not all. There was something else which worried Owl. As they were coming indoors, he was sure he had caught sight of that dog, lurking round the corner. He thought it had followed them home, and now it knew where they lived.

Robbie was very sorry to hear the story.

'Real dogs aren't always like that,' he said.

'No, I know,' said Owl, 'but you have to be a bit careful with real animals. I think this is the one everyone has been talking about. And it's true – it *is* horrible and dangerous.'

'I shouldn't think Katy will be allowed to go out on her own until it's gone,' said Jinny anxiously. 'I hope she isn't, especially if it's hanging around.'

'I think I know what it wants,' said Ginger mysteriously. 'It's obvious when you think about it.'

'What? What do you mean?' asked all the toys.

'It has come –' Ginger paused dramatically, ' – to steal Jinny the Guinea's tail!'

'Oh, stop it,' said Jinny. 'You know I haven't got a tail. Stop making jokes about it.'

'OK, OK. Keep your tail on,' said Ginger.

They had begun to get over their fright and started to talk about other things. But in an odd sort of way, Ginger was about to be proved right.

The weather was very fine, and everyone was busy for most of the day. Katy played complicated games in the garden and the toys hardly had a moment to think. Ginger managed a few tricks, of course. She always found time for that. When it was very hot, Katy was allowed to have the garden hose on and she kept the paddling pool filled with water. Mouse had been balanced on the edge of the pool, when Ginger crept up behind him and said, 'Wotcher, mate!' in a strange, deep voice. Mouse had jumped so high he slipped in the pool. Worse still, Mrs Henrietta James had been resting on the lawn when Ginger had pretended to fall over the garden hose. As it snaked up, Ginger had helped it in the direction of Mrs Henrietta, and she had been drenched. She positively shrieked.

'Careless cat! Criminal cat !'

'Go and drip somewhere else, there's a treasure,' said Ginger calmly.

As she and Mouse had to spend the night in the airing cupboard to dry off, they were all reminded of the ghost incident, as well as the shark, so no one was very pleased with Ginger.

Robbie tried to talk to her, but she just said, 'Got to liven the old place up a bit, Robbie lad.'

The days became even hotter, and it stayed so hot that Katy was allowed to play outside until quite late. Ginger began to get on everyone's nerves. When they had supper on the lawn, she dipped their straws into bubble-blowing mixture and then put them back in the mugs of orange juice. It went all frothy and bubbled, and they all shouted 'Yuck!' and pulled faces.

As it began to get dark, she went to Katy's mother's bag and took out a ball of yellow wool, stuck it on a knitting needle and propped it up in the sandpit. Then she told Bear there was a girl called Goldilocks waiting to see him. He went all the way down to the sandpit before he could see it was a trick. In fact, if it had not been for Katy's mother clearing up the garden before she went to bed, Bear might have been left out all night – Katy was getting quite careless. She went to bed very late now, and it was easy to forget about putting the toys away. It was dry at night too, so that even Katy's mother began to forget. When this finally happened, the toys did not really mind. It was a bit like camping, lying outside looking at the stars. They felt quite safe in the garden with its tall, wooden fence and the strong garden gate. Until, that is, a visitor came late in the evening, and when he left, he did not shut the gate.

That particular night, Robbie and Ginger came in early. They had been out in the car that afternoon, and Katy's mother carried them in when she brought home the shopping. Katy was playing with Jinny and Bear outside, and she had put Jinny on the swing and forgotten her. The visitor had come and he sat in the garden with Katy's parents, drinking coffee. It was quite dark when he left and although he banged the gate behind him, it had not shut.

It was hardly possible to see the dark shadow which slipped inside the gate, paused, then moved silently along the path. It crossed the grass and disappeared for a moment behind the rose trees. The shadow did not go near the chairs where Katy's parents had sat. They were near the house, and the shadow skirted the pool of light thrown from behind the glass doors which were slightly open. It liked the dark best, it seemed. It approached the swing, sniffing here and there. It passed right under the swing, but touched the seat as it passed and Jinny fell off. Instantly, the shadow pounced and Jinny was carried swiftly away out of the garden.

Robbie was woken up by a strange noise outside the door. A scratching, scrabbling noise, and what sounded like crying and gasping at the same time. He opened the door and Bear fell inside.

'Bear! What is it? What's happened?'

'Jinny. It's Jinny. She's gone.'

'Look, sit down, Bear. You look terrible. Try and tell me slowly.'

Ginger appeared and stared at Bear, who was just sitting there looking very frightened indeed.

'Oh, Robbie,' he said. 'It was awful. I was sitting on the chairs outside the glass doors when I saw something come in the gate. It was very big but very quiet. I couldn't see it properly but it seemed to be searching. I kept very still. Then it came across in front of the doors. It looked in my direction. I thought it had seen me because it showed its teeth. Great fangs they were. Really horrible. But it wouldn't come near the light. Then it went towards the swing. Jinny was there. It knocked Jinny off the swing, and then I saw her. She was being carried off in its horrible teeth!'

Bear began to cry again.

'I didn't know what to do. I took a

chance, and slipped through the glass doors to come and tell you.'

'I must go out at once,' said Robbie, looking very agitated.

'You can't,' said Ginger. 'The doors will be locked by now. There's only one thing to do. We must find Owl. There might be an open window. He must carry out a night search and find Jinny before it's too late.'

CHAPTER SIX

Owl's Night Adventure

Owl never minded being out in the dark. He preferred it to the daytime. Now he was flying in the warm streaming air, over the gardens, and over trees that lined the avenue. They had worked out the shadow would take the easiest route if it was carrying something, so he was going to watch the roads. He was at least ten minutes behind, of course, so it would be difficult at the crossroads. On the other hand, searching from the air was always an advantage. He could see a great deal, as long as the creature did not go under cover. Bear had said that it had four legs and awful teeth. They had all guessed what it

74

was, of course: the dog. That dreadful
dog which had attacked them and
then followed them home. Owl remembered its teeth, too. That strange wild
dog had snatched Jinny, and was now
running to its hide-out.

Owl was approaching the crossroads. He began to lose height and
settled on a telegraph pole. He looked
up and down the main road, but there
was nothing, except, occasionally, car
headlights sweeping the grass verge.
No one there. He looked up and down
the other road. He had already trav-
elled along half of it, and there was

no sign of anything on the far side. He suddenly realized how difficult his task was. He had flown straight to the crossroads – but what if their enemy had gone the other way, straight out to the open country? He had no means of knowing. He looked across over the streets and houses in despair. Jinny could have been taken into any of the gardens, and many of them were well-sheltered with trees and shrubs. He saw a straight line in the distance, the old railway line. There was an old signal box by the line, and his keen eyes observed a movement there. Could this be what he was looking for? It was an ideal hide-out, miles from anywhere, and deserted now that the railway no longer ran. He took off again, flying swiftly and strongly towards the hut.

As he approached, he could see no further sign of movement. There was no wind, and the moon's light was cold. It was a strange, still picture and Owl felt nervous, although he could see nothing wrong. He circled a little and then, seeing a window in the roof, dropped lightly down beside it. He peered through the dirty glass, trying to see into the darkness. As he reached forward, a strong movement from behind flipped him on to his back and he was pinned to the roof, looking up at the moon. He could only think of those teeth and closed his eyes, but the next thing he heard was a harsh voice saying, 'Password?'

Owl opened his eyes. He was indeed facing a real animal, but this was a cat – much larger than Ginger – with fierce, piercing eyes. Owl wished he was at home with Katy. The cat sniffed at him and seemed puzzled. He called out.

'Old Grey! You had better come. I thought I had caught an owl, but it smells all wrong.'

A huge grey cat appeared and looked down at Owl.

'He was spying on us,' said the guard.

The old cat looked at him carefully.

'This is a toy owl,' he said. 'A harmless creature, but it has no business here. Release him.'

Owl got up feeling very shaky.

'I wasn't spying,' he insisted. 'I am looking for a friend. She has been stolen and we are very frightened for her.' His voice wobbled a little, but he managed to get the whole story out, and the cats listened in silence.

By now, there were many cats surrounding him and Owl realized that he had interrupted something important. For some reason, a large number of cats had been gathered in this place. Old Grey explained:

'We prepare for the Great Council in two days' time. Come in, and we will discuss your case.'

Inside, Owl was astonished to see cats everywhere. They packed the signal box, and were all sizes and colours. In the darkness, many pairs of eyes stared at him. They made way for Old Grey who leaped on to the table and began to talk. He told Owl's story and, when he had finished, added:

'The little owl believes he may have seen the creature before. A few days ago he was attacked by a wild and ferocious dog, a big yellowy-coloured dog.'

The cats began to growl in their throats.

'We know him,' they cried. 'He is our enemy.'

Old Grey nodded.

'He injured a young cat recently. He is dangerous.'

Owl felt very cold, his own danger forgotten. Poor Jinny! They must find her quickly. It might be too late already.

'Please help me,' he shouted. 'I must rescue my friend.'

'You are not of our kind,' said a striped cat. 'Why should we run into trouble for you?'

'I don't know,' said Owl honestly, 'but I'm very afraid for my friend.'

He looked anxiously at the old cat.

'Perhaps we could assist in some minor way,' conceded Old Grey.

'We can assist,' said the striped cat, 'but we should not get involved. We are not dogs and we are not toys.'

A black cat with beautiful long fur stood up.

'I think we should show him where the Yellow lives. We need not get involved, but we can lead him to his companion. Will you come with me, Stripe?'

The striped cat did not answer, but an elegant Siamese cat jumped lightly to the floor.

'I will come with you, Black, but we must go at once. It will soon be light.'

Old Grey would not permit Owl to go, so he waited anxiously while the big cat explained that Black and Siam would travel quickly and secretly to the old railway station. The building was deserted and partly boarded up, but the dog had made it his lair. At night, he roamed the countryside, only rarely venturing out during the day. In two days, it would be the night of the Great Council of All Cats, and they intended to post a guard round the old station to make sure the dog did not disturb them. They called him the Yellow and many cats feared him.

Owl listened and felt very afraid for Jinny. Poor little Jinny, she must be terrified. He almost hoped she was not there, after all; but he knew that Bear's shadowy creature with fearful teeth, the dreadful wild dog he had seen, and the cats' Yellow must be the same animal.

When the two cats returned, they were agitated but triumphant. They paced about, lashing their tails, and described how they had approached the old railway station warily, soon discovering that the Yellow had returned.

'We could hear him,' said Black. 'He has made a den in the big room where passengers used to wait. There are windows on one side, boarded up, and a door. The door is broken at the top, but a big animal – or a cat – can get over it. That is how the dog gets in and out.'

'On the other side,' said Siam, 'is a high, broken window, with the sloping roof of an office right underneath. I looked in at the window and he saw me. He's ferocious. He jumped at the window again and again, barking and growling and snapping.'

'And I slipped round to the other side and jumped on the door,' said Black. 'I couldn't see Jinny at first, then she moved.'

'Is she all right?' asked Owl quickly.

'She seemed unharmed. She moved fast.'

'Poor Jinny,' whispered Owl. 'She isn't very brave.'

'She's got brains,' replied Black. 'She took the chance we gave her. There's a lot of rubbish in the old fireplace. She scrambled up the rubbish and into the chimney. She can't climb up, of course, but if she's on the first ledge, the Yellow can't get at her. He's too big.'

'He was absolutely mad,' added Siam, 'but there's bad news, too. He has a mate. She almost got us. They must take it in turns to go out, so no chance of rescuing her when the Yellow goes in search of food. Sorry.'

Owl suddenly felt very tired.

'You must go quickly,' said Old Grey. 'It is nearly morning.'

'Thank you for your help,' said Owl quietly. 'At least we know she's all right, and we know where she is.'

Black and Old Grey walked outside with him. 'Good luck,' shouted Black.

Owl beat his way wearily home.

'There must be something we can do,' he said to himself, 'but the dog is so strong, and we are so weak.'

Then, as he began the drop to Katy's house, he shouted out fiercely, 'But we *will* rescue her. We *will*!'

CHAPTER SEVEN

Council of Cats

The house was very quiet the next day. Owl was sleeping. He had been able to tell the others about his search and the meeting with the cats, but was too exhausted to answer any questions. It was just as well that Katy was at school all day. They just wanted to stay indoors. They were all very upset. Mouse kept bursting into squeaky little tears, and Mrs Henrietta James was surprisingly kind and sensible with him.

'Chin up, Mouse,' she said. 'We must be brave for Jinny's sake. You'll see, we'll win through in the end. Keep your pecker up. Oh, you haven't got a pecker,' she added.

They all knew Bear was worried. He wasn't eating at all. Robbie paced up and down. He had not slept much. Ginger disappeared for most of the day. She did not play one single trick. As it grew dark, they all gathered round the kitchen table, and Owl told his story again.

'You were brave when the cats caught you,' said Mouse.

'Not really,' said Owl. 'I was too shocked. They were quite kind but they feel it's not their business. And the dogs are dangerous.'

'So it's up to us,' said Robbie. 'Let's work out a plan.'

'It's a long way to the old railway station,' said Mouse. 'We'd need a rest when we got there.'

'We need to be able to climb, too,' said Bear. 'I think I can, but I'm a bit out of practice.'

'We also need to create a diversion.' Robbie was thinking out loud. 'You know, someone must attract the dogs' attention while someone else rescues Jinny.'

'We can't do it,' said Ginger, speaking for the first time. 'There are too few of us. And as for climbing and creating diversions, some of you can't even run! Don't you realize? These are two ferocious dogs!'

No one spoke. It was true, of course. They were used to a quiet, indoor life. This would be a desperate adventure.

'There's only one thing to do,' said Robbie. 'I must persuade the cats to help. I will go to their Council.'

'Robbie!' said Owl anxiously. 'You're a dog. They certainly won't listen to you. They didn't really accept me. Besides, you may not get a chance to speak to them. They may think you're the enemy.'

'Don't go, Robbie dear,' clucked Mrs Henrietta. 'Please don't run into danger deliberately.'

'We'd be no use without you, Robbie,' added Bear.

Owl stood up suddenly.

'Ginger must go,' he said.

Everyone turned to look at Ginger. She said nothing. She did not blink, but her tail was twitching at the end.

'That makes sense,' agreed Mouse. 'You are a cat.'

Ginger spat fiercely.

'Not a real cat, stupid! They wouldn't take any notice of me. I don't belong to their Council. Their families are not my families.' She turned her back on them.

'I shall go.' Robbie broke the silence. 'We must try. If I fail with the cats, then we will have a go on our own. If I don't come back . . .' He paused and cleared his throat. 'I will expect Ginger to lead a rescue.'

Ginger did not turn round.

'Now,' said Robbie, briskly. 'I must make my plans. The Council meets tomorrow night. I shall have to go before the doors are locked. I can't get through windows like Owl. You must make me a map of the route, Owl. I'll go to the cross-roads, like you, and then cut across the fields. But first of all, we must get some sleep.'

The following day was long and difficult. In the evening, Robbie waited as
long as he dared, then slipped out of
the glass doors into the garden. As he
wriggled under the gate, he heard the
doors being closed behind him. He
wondered how he would get back.
There was some cloud and the moonlight was occasionally blotted out.
Robbie padded along the road, looking neither left nor right. He was not a
nervous animal, but he rarely ven-
tured out at night and the shadows
confused him. He hoped he would not
meet any cats before he got to the
meeting place. He hoped he would not
meet the Yellow at all.

At the crossroads he paused and
tried to remember Owl's drawing. He
thought he heard a soft noise behind
him, but when he turned there was
nothing. He could smell a freshness in
the air over towards the fields and
knew he must go in that direction. He

moved more quickly, his shadow running beside him now. He could hear that noise again, a padding noise, not unlike his own paws on the road. Perhaps it was an echo? He ran a little faster, and then faster as the noise increased, until he was almost galloping. Then he saw it. There were two shadows running beside him, and only one was his.

'Hello, old mate,' said Ginger's voice. 'Thought I'd come out for a run. Nice night.'

Robbie smiled to himself and, feeling more hopeful than he had been for a long time, he galloped on with his friend Ginger running beside him, in the direction of the old railway line.

Neither of them spoke again until they were approaching the old signal box, then Ginger began to talk.

'I think you had better hide in the bushes, while I go forward on my own. I'll try and get inside and talk to them. If things go well, I'll send for

you. If not, well, don't wait after sunrise.'

'We'll see how it goes,' said Robbie, 'but I agree. Better for them to see you first.'

Robbie dropped back as they reached the last scrubby bushes, while Ginger ran on and leaped on to the low, lean-to roof beside the signal box. She meant to find out what she could before declaring herself, but the cats were too well organized. In the bushes, Robbie felt a heavy weight land on his shoulders. As he sank

down, he felt sharp claws in the back
of his neck. On the roof, Ginger was
faring no better than little Owl. She
was helpless on her back, a strong
paw pinning her down and sharp
teeth inches from her throat. Ginger
thought quickly, then she decided.

'Don't TICKLE!' she said. 'And
take your dirty paw off my lovely
white bib.'

The guard cat was surprised. He
was a good fighter, but his opponents
did not usually say things like this.
He drew back a little, very cautiously.
Ginger was on her feet in a flash.

'Now look here, my treasure,' she
said to the guard. 'Just toddle off and
get your grandad. You know, the grey
one.'

'Old Grey?' replied the guard. 'You
ask to see Old Grey?'

'You're a quick lad,' said Ginger
kindly. 'I knew I could rely on you.
Off you go.'

Ginger could see there were other
cats all around her. She waved a

vague paw.

'Hi there, guys. Sunday School is it? Snooker night? Sorry to interrupt. Urgent business with Old Grey.'

'Someone had better fetch him,' said a thin black-and-white cat. 'It seems to be a cat, yet it is not a cat.' He sniffed Ginger in a puzzled way.

'Cheeky!' said Ginger. 'You'd smell funny if you'd been in the washing machine as often as I have.'

The younger cats gasped in horror, but the guards held the circle round her until Old Grey appeared. He looked at Ginger and sighed.

'So,' he said, 'another toy. You are a friend of the little owl, I can guess. And did you bring a dog with you?'

'Well, I did, just a bit,' said Ginger, crouching respectfully. 'Lovely chap, he is. You'll adore him.'

'This creature is quite mad,' said Old Grey. 'Bring them both into the Council Chamber.'

Ginger and Robbie stood side by side. Like Owl, they saw more cats than they knew existed. They filled the old signal box, perched on ledges, covering the floor, all waiting quietly. Old Grey scratched three times on the table.

'The Council recommences,' he announced, 'but we have extra business.' He turned to Ginger and Robbie. 'This is a secret Council. You have no right to be here. Explain yourselves.'

Robbie and Ginger looked at each other. Robbie nodded slightly, so Ginger began.

'Thank you for having us. This is really kind. You already know half our business. Our friend Jinny is being held prisoner by the Yellow. We cannot rescue her on our own, so we have come to you. We know how clever you are, how brave, how noble—'

'Enough nonsense!' snarled the striped cat. 'We told the owl. It is not our affair. You are not of our kind. There is no reason why we should help you.'

'Stripe is right,' confirmed Old Grey. 'You have no call on us. The Yellow and his mate are dangerous. I cannot ask my people to go into danger for a matter which is not their concern.'

'But it is !' cried Ginger. 'I am a cat, and Jinny is my friend. She is my family. Robbie is a dog, but Jinny is his family too. The Yellow is bad. He frightens and hurts people. He has even hurt one of your cats. We should all join together and defeat him. What does it matter if we are a bit different? We should look after each other.'

There was silence in the room. Then Old Grey said, 'Who wishes to speak?'

Siam stepped forward.

'The ginger cat is right. I am different from many of you, but I am still a cat. We have often worked together.'

There was a murmur of agreement.

'I support Siam.' Black stood up. 'The ginger cat speaks of friendship. It is true. At home, my friend is an old mother dog. She looked after me when

I was a kitten. Now she is old, I protect her.'

'Rubbish!' shouted Stripe. 'Be friends if you wish, but the Yellow could kill any of us. Shall we risk that for a toy guinea-pig and a noisy ginger half-cat?'

'Come here and say that,' Ginger shouted back, 'you moth-eaten, flea-ridden, striped pair of fur pyjamas!'

There was a shocked silence. Stripe was not the biggest cat, but he was the strongest and fiercest. But still, striped pair of fur pyjamas! Robbie, crouched on the floor, realized that the rustle of little noises which followed meant that some cats were laughing. He stood up.

'Have I permission to speak?'

Old Grey nodded.

'We have come to you,' explained Robbie, 'because the Yellow is our common enemy. He holds prisoner a very dear friend of ours, and we cannot rescue her without your help. If you refuse, we shall still try, but we are not strong. Apart from Ginger and Owl, we have Mouse, Bear and – well – a hen.'

'Good gracious!' exclaimed Old Grey. 'You intend to march on the Yellow with an army like that!'

The room was in uproar. Siam's high voice made itself heard.

'That settles it!' he said. 'I won't have anyone saying that a mouse is braver than I am!'

'And a hen!' said Black. 'A hen going into battle for her friend while cats sit on one side! I'm going, too. A vote! A vote!'

'Very well.' Old Grey scratched three times on the table. 'Do we go?'

One great yowl filled the room. Robbie's hair stood on end.

'And you, Stripe? You do not vote.'

Stripe stood up.

'It is clear,' he hissed, 'that the ginger lump of stuffing should have someone to guard her during this enterprise. Otherwise, she could bring disaster on us all. I will go.'

'Then it is decided. Generals, come to the table. The battle begins tomorrow night!'

CHAPTER EIGHT

Preparations

Robbie and Ginger hardly noticed the journey back. They were full of excitement. It had been nerve-wracking at the Council, but once planning began the cats were very efficient. Robbie was worried that Jinny would be so frightened that she would not be able to help herself. What if she wouldn't come out of the chimney? Siam had suggested that Owl should try and make first contact. He could land on the chimney and if it was not possible to talk to her, he would have to try dropping a note. There was a lot more to tell the others. They must get back as soon as possible.

As they skidded in at the garden

gate, Robbie remembered the locked door. How was he going to get in? They went straight to the glass doors, and saw Bear faithfully watching and waiting. He waved and pointed to the high open window that Ginger had used. The next moment, Owl came out through the window and fluttered down. He was carrying the end of a piece of string.

'Are you both all right? Bear has worked out a way of getting Robbie back. We've got to get a bucket from the sandpit.'

Robbie ran to the sandpit and knocked the sand out of the largest bucket. Owl explained:

'We have to tie the string to the handle; then if Robbie gets into the bucket, I'll go back through the window with the string, and we'll all haul him up.'

'Right,' said Ginger. 'I'd better go in as well and help.'

She jumped on to the back of the garden seat, up to the window and disappeared inside. Owl followed. Indoors, Bear had tied the end of the string to the leg of the table, just in case, and all the animals lined up and began to haul on the string.

'Heave-ho my hearties, dears,' said Mrs Henrietta, as Robbie rose slowly into the air.

With some difficulty they got him level with the open window.

'Ah,' murmured Bear, 'oh dear. I haven't thought how to get him down on this side.'

Robbie scrambled out of the bucket, and got his paws on the window frame. He balanced there, scrabbling wildly.

'Quick,' said Mouse, 'get the cushion from the armchair to break his fall.'

Mrs Henrietta and Owl dragged the fat cushion on to the floor and got it under the window just in time. With one last scrabble, Robbie lost his balance and fell forward safely on to the cushion. The bucket followed him, hitting Mrs Henrietta squarely on the back.

'Oof!' gasped Mrs Henrietta, and laid a ping-pong ball.

They all rushed quickly into the toy cupboard and shut the door. Katy was going to be puzzled about the bucket, but they had more important things to worry about. Strangely enough, they felt quite cheerful. Their success with the window seemed a good sign, and the fact that the cats were going to help was wonderful news. They sat round the kitchen table again and listened to Robbie.

'It's tomorrow night. First of all, the cats will send out scouts,' he explained. 'They will discover exactly where both dogs are. Owl will go with them and try and get in touch with Jinny. He will be quite safe if he doesn't get near the ground. If one of the dogs goes out, a group of cats will follow and prevent its return while the rest of us rescue Jinny. If the dogs are both there, it will be a little more difficult. In that case, we will all be needed at the old railway station.'

Ginger turned to Mouse.

'We would like you to be our messenger. Someone must keep in touch with Headquarters. Perhaps Mrs Henrietta will help you in the signal box.'

Mouse agreed at once, but Mrs Henrietta James said:

'Don't worry about me, dears. I'll make myself useful.'

'The rest of us will go to the station. Is everyone clear?'

They nodded but Bear looked worried.

'There's just one thing, Robbie. How shall we all get out of the house tonight?'

They all looked at each other.

'Well, Mrs Henrietta and I can fly, and Ginger can jump,' said Owl. 'One of us could manage Mouse as well, but Robbie and Bear are too heavy.'

'Can we use the string and bucket again?' asked Bear.

'I don't think we can,' answered Robbie. 'It needs you to be there, pulling the string. You're the strongest.'

They were quiet again, because everyone was thinking.

'We could get out one by one after Katy has gone to bed. The doors are usually open until quite late. If we go separately, we should be able to do it without being noticed.' Robbie was thinking aloud.

'We would need somewhere to hide until we were all together,' warned Mouse. 'Otherwise, Katy's mother might tidy us away again.'

'I know,' said Robbie. 'There's Katy's old pram in the garage. They can't shut the garage door, it's too full of junk, and the pram is right at the back. No one looks at it these days.'

'Good thinking, Batdog,' said Ginger. 'It's exactly right with the hood and cover, and there's room for us all.'

'And how shall we get back, dears?' asked Mrs Henrietta James.

'Oh, let's face that when the time

comes,' said Ginger impatiently. 'I'll think of something. If necessary, I'll shout "Fire!" Then you can rush in when they all rush out.'

'Really!' said Robbie. 'I hope you can come up with something better than that.'

By evening, they were all ready. As it happened, there was no problem for Mrs Henrietta James and Bear. Katy had taken them out to the garden so, at bedtime, they slipped down behind the chairs and were not taken indoors. When it was safe, they hurried across to the garage and had no trouble clambering over the cardboard boxes and into the pram. Mouse arrived next. Bear leaned over and hauled him in by his tail. The pram rocked violently when Ginger sprang up, and they also had to give Robbie a bit of a hand. It was getting a little crowded under the cover now.

'Move up. Spread out a bit,' complained Ginger, and they all shuffled along.

'Ugh! Yuck!' screeched Mrs Henrietta. 'It's all damp at this end.' And they all rushed back to the dry end.

'I feel seasick,' groaned Mouse. 'Can't you all stop bouncing about?'

'Reminds me of Sardines,' murmured Ginger. 'I know a good spooky story. Want to hear it?'

'No!' they all said.

'Spoilsports,' said Ginger, and, wrapping her tail round her, she settled down to sleep.

It was dark when Robbie woke them. They climbed down from the pram and made their way carefully to the gate. They all slipped under except Bear, who stuck halfway. It seemed for a moment that there might be a problem, but Ginger solved it by doing a quick bounce on Bear's round tummy while Robbie and Owl pulled his legs.

'Ouch!' yelled Bear, but he was through.

Once outside, they began to feel

excited. Mouse climbed up on Robbie's back and they began to move quickly. Mrs Henrietta James could fly quite well in a series of long flutters. By the time they reached the old signal box they were breathless, but ready to go on and do whatever had to be done.

This time, the cats were waiting.

'Password?' shouted the guard.

'Fur pyjamas,' replied Ginger rudely, and all the guards roared happily.

Siam came out to meet them and took them all straight into the signal box. Mouse stayed on Robbie's back. He felt hot and cold by turns. There were cats everywhere he looked. Old Grey came down the steps leading up to the signals, and Ginger introduced them all. Old Grey was especially careful to welcome Mouse and Mrs Henrietta. Mouse looked nervous, but Mrs Henrietta seemed quite unworried and rather perky.

'So kind of you, dear,' she said to

Old Grey, just as if she had been invited to tea. 'I'm looking forward to our little excitement.'

'Quite so, Madam, but please do not run into any danger. You must leave all that to us. I wondered, in fact, if you and Mouse would care to remain here and prepare a meal? We shall need it on our return. And you will be here if messengers are needed.'

Mouse was only too pleased to agree. The cats alarmed him as much as the thought of the dogs did. Old Grey turned to the others.

'Bear will be most helpful to us tonight. We need someone to push the window open when Siam leads the diversion on the roof. Will you go with him?'

'The scouts are ready to go,' shouted a voice from outside.

'That's you, Owl,' said Old Grey. 'Try and talk to Jinny, and then come straight back. Later, your job will be to keep contact between myself and the two leaders, Siam and Black.'

The scouts set off at a good pace, fanning out as they approached the railway station so that they could all creep up on it from a different direction. Overhead, they could see Owl, flying strongly in the moonlight. Old Grey turned back to his task.

'Now you, Robbie. Will you go with Black? She's leading the attacking party. Siam's group will create a diversion at the window on the left. Black's party will do the same at the door. You may have to go in, but I hope not.'

'What about me?' asked Ginger.

'You and Stripe have a special duty. You must be quick and agile. The old booking office adjoins the room where the dogs are. The door is locked, but there is a small hole where the tickets used to be sold and you and Stripe are small enough to get through. The dogs probably don't know it's there. Wait until they are fully occupied with the attack from the window and door, then go in. You, Ginger, pick up

Jinny and return the same way, and Stripe will hold the dogs off until you're through. He will then make his own escape.'

'That sounds very risky,' said Robbie.

'This adventure is not without danger,' replied Old Grey, 'but you know that.'

Several voices were heard outside and the door flew open.

'The scouts are back,' shouted a guard.

They hurried out, and Robbie was relieved to see Owl arriving first.

'Bad news!' he gasped.

The leader of the scouts ran up.

'Bad news, sir. Both the Yellow and his mate are there. The mate has only just come back and I'm sure they've already eaten, so I don't think either one will be leaving tonight.'

'That makes our task more difficult, but we were prepared for this. And you, Owl?'

'I couldn't make contact with

Jinny,' said Owl unhappily. 'The Yellow kept looking into the fireplace so I couldn't call to her, and there's no possibility of anything else. The chimney's blocked. There's only the tiniest of holes.'

'This is unfortunate,' said Old Grey, beginning to pace up and down. 'It means that Stripe must hold them long enough for Ginger to persuade Jinny to come out, and she'll be very frightened. Siam's cats will be making a terrible racket.'

'I'll go,' said Mouse.

'I beg your pardon?' said Old Grey.

'I'll go and tell her. I'm the smallest one here. I'll try and creep across the floor without them noticing.'

'Bless his little heart,' said Mrs Henrietta James.

'I really admire you, kid,' said Ginger, 'I really do. But they would be bound to sense that you were there.'

'I know!' said Bear, suddenly. 'What about my idea with the string? Is the hole in the chimney big enough for Mouse?'

'Well, yes,' said Owl. 'Mouse could get through.'

'String!' shouted Ginger, jumping about. 'String, string. Find some string.'

'Will someone explain?' asked Old Grey.

'It's simple,' said Bear. 'We tie a piece of string to Mouse's tail and Owl will lower him down the chimney.'

One of the cats had found some string wound round a wooden post and was biting it free. They took two bits and tied them together.

'What if it's too short?' asked Robbie doubtfully.

'It will be more than halfway,' said Mouse. 'Just let go. Then, when the time comes –' Mouse shut his eyes '– Stripe can bring me out.'

'Actually,' said Ginger to the astonished cats, 'my friend Mouse is really a famous circus performer. When he's not on the trapeze, he wrestles with tigers. Hop on my back, old mate, I'll give you a ride to the station.'

'Yes, we must go.' Old Grey called the cats to order and gave them their last instructions: 'Do your best,' he said, 'and good luck.'

The scouts reported the way ahead clear, and the cats melted into the countryside. Only Owl was visible in the moonlight, and no one had remembered Mrs Henrietta James. She stood by the door waiting until even

Owl was out of sight.

'Well,' she clucked, 'so I'm supposed to stay here and make all these fishpaste sandwiches! What old-fashioned fuddy-duddies they are. Henrietta, my dear, it's time you prepared for take-off!'

CHAPTER NINE

The Battle

Robbie crouched quietly in the bushes near the old railway station for the second time. On the last occasion there had been an enemy on his back. This time he was shoulder to shoulder with the same cats, and they were going to rescue Jinny together. Robbie wondered what Katy would think if she knew: that morning, she had spent a lot of time looking for Jinny.

'She must be here,' her mother had told her. 'You must have a good tidy-up at the weekend. No wonder you can't find anything.'

Robbie sighed. Where would Jinny be by then?

Mouse was flying. He had never wished to fly, never wished to lead an exciting life, yet here he was. Rising swiftly, he was approaching the chimney on top of the old railway station. When they had talked about how to get him there, Owl had been very tactful about it, explaining that owls could carry mice in their talons on certain occasions.

'You know,' said Ginger, 'bank holidays, birthdays, weddings, funerals. Special occasions.'

'Particularly funerals, I suppose,' said Mouse. 'Thank you very much.' But he trusted Owl. It was the escape with Stripe he feared.

They landed lightly on the chimney. Mouse unwound the string from around his middle. He looked like a very small mountaineer. The string was already tied to his tail and Owl wound it firmly round his claw.

'Are you ready, Mouse?' whispered Owl.

'All set. Lower away,' Mouse

replied softly.

At the blockage, halfway down the chimney, he slipped through with some difficulty, but then continued down in complete, thick darkness. Soon there was no more string. He swung for a few moments, waiting for Owl to let go, but nothing happened. How could he tell Owl? Suddenly, he panicked. Twisting up the string, he bit through it. The weight gone, Owl fell backwards off the chimney pot and had to flap hard to regain his balance. Mouse plunged down, not very far, and landed on a soft cushion, which said 'Oof!' in Jinny's voice.

'It's me, it's me!' he squeaked.

'Is that Mouse?' asked Jinny, quietly. 'I knew someone would come.'

'It's the beginning of the rescue,' Mouse whispered back. 'I've got to tell you all about it, then we must be ready.'

Up on the outhouse roof, Siam had already leaped lightly into position and was stalking towards the window. Bear was standing on an old water barrel and getting a bit of a bunk-up from two of the guards. Soon, the whole party was up on the roof, watching Siam at the window. He slipped back and reported:

'The Yellow and his mate are both there. The mate is lying down. She may be asleep but I'm not sure. Old Yellow is prowling about, though. He's snuffling at the fireplace. I fear he may have heard something. Bear, you come over to the window and open it as quietly as possible.'

Bear dropped down on all fours and found he could manage much better like that. He followed Siam carefully. The window was partly broken. Bear could see, if he got a good grip on it, the window would open outwards. He braced himself, and very, very quietly began to pull, but it did not move. He took a deep breath and pulled harder. In a rush, the frame jerked out with a scraping sound and Bear slid on the tiles. They all froze. The Yellow stopped snuffling. He was listening, too. After a moment, Siam nodded, and Bear took the rest of the frame back on its hinges so that the window stood completely open. They slipped back to the others.

'Get ready,' ordered Siam. 'As soon as we receive the signal, we want as many heads in that window as possible, all at once and screeching loudly. Bear, report back to Old Grey and tell him we are ready.'

Bear scrambled into the bushes with his news. His part was done and Black's group now prepared to go forward. He smiled at Robbie and raised a paw. Robbie nodded and padded off with the cats. Owl, watching from the roof, waited to perform his last task. The outhouse roof was quiet but he could see dark shapes on the tiles, gathered round the gaping hole where the window had been. He looked out towards the railway line and saw a shadow moving across the ground.

He glanced at the moon but no cloud was passing. He looked back at the shadow which still advanced. He could see now. It was a great mass of cats, moving in formation towards him.

'They're coming!' thought Owl. 'They're coming!'

As they approached the station, they divided, taking up positions on either side of the door. Owl saw a flash of white and realized Robbie was there among the dark cats. He waited until the cats stopped moving and then gave two long hoots.

The effect was dreadful! The cats on the roof began to screech and howl. Siam's voice was particularly loud. The two dogs were plunged from complete silence into a deafening racket of enemy noise. They looked up and saw the window crowded with yowling heads. Again and again, they leaped at the window, but it was too high. Even Ginger and Stripe, crouched on the narrow ledge of the ticket counter,

looked at each other, and Ginger pressed a paw against her ear. The dogs were barking too and it hardly seemed possible that there could be more noise but, at a signal from Black, a group of cats and Robbie hurled themselves at the broken door and set up another appalling din. The dogs were confused. They ran between the door and the window, leaping and snapping. Ginger and Stripe took the chance to slip through the little arch, where previously only tickets and moncy had passed, and crouched on the counter. If they could get down before they were seen, they stood a better chance.

Black jumped on to the top of the broken door and spat defiantly. The Yellow rushed at her and, for a few moments, he was entirely absorbed, leaping at her from his side of the door while Black leaped from the other side. Ginger, seeing her chance, dropped to the floor and raced to the fireplace. The Yellow hurled himself at the half-door so hard it gave way, and he burst outside. Immediately a half-circle of cats closed round. Mad with anger, he saw a black-and-white creature on the far side, a kind of dog and yet not a dog. He crouched low and sprang.

'Run!' yelled Black. 'Run, Robbie! Lead him away.'

And Robbie ran for his life.

He first ran straight across to the bushes, and then remembered Bear and the others waiting there. He swung round, heading for the open countryside, and saw the Yellow turn too – despite the harassment from Black and her cats. He began to falter. He was no match for a large angry dog. He had run about as far as he could. Just then, Robbie saw the second group of cats – Black's reserves. They were headed by Old Grey himself, and were coming between him and the Yellow. The big dog hesitated. The yowling pack on his tail held back, but the new horde kept coming and they were horribly silent. The Yellow turned and streaked towards the old railway line which led to the safety of the town.

In the waiting-room, the Yellow's mate stood staring at the fireplace, ears back. She had realized that she would never reach the cats at the window and was prepared to follow her mate. But, there in the fireplace, was a small ginger cat with a strange, dirty, bedraggled creature in its mouth. Here were easy victims. As she shuffled forward, another cat leaped down in front of her. It was not much larger, but it was fierce and smelled like the enemy. It wasted no time in slashing its claws in her direction.

Ginger moved. Up to the counter she jumped, through the arch, and deposited Jinny on the ledge. They looked back through the glass: Stripe and the dog were fighting, and the cat looked very small.

'Wait here, Jinny,' Ginger panted. 'I'm going back for Mouse.'

'Don't go in there, Ginger,' said Jinny, horrified. 'You can't go back.'

But Ginger was already through.

Siam, from above, had already realized Stripe's danger, and had sent his cats scrambling frantically down to get round to the door. They all knew it had been the plan to distract the dogs. Once any of them had to get inside the room, it was only too possible that someone would get hurt. Siam was bracing himself. He looked down at the unequal struggle, saw Ginger pick up Mouse and, with an ear-splitting screech, hurtled down on to the dog. Stripe was backing into a corner. With Siam's help, he might get out, but not, it seemed, without injury. He could hear Ginger shouting,

'This way, Stripe. I've got Mouse. Get to the counter.'

But how? Just then, he heard a squawk and a flutter. Something was flying overhead. It banked steeply and zoomed down on the dog.

'Bombs away, dears,' it said, and a

small but heavy jar of fishpaste dropped from above on to the dog's head. Mrs Henrietta James had made herself useful.

It was too much. With a howl of fright, the dog turned and raced out of the open door. It was faced by an army of cats returning from the railway line. The Yellow's mate gave up entirely and fled into the countryside.

Old Grey hurried into the waiting-room.

'Is everyone all right?' he asked.

'My group is OK,' said Siam.'Stripe here has been cut, but it's not bad.'

Old Grey looked up at the counter. Sitting on it were a ginger cat, a very dirty guinea-pig, a soot-covered mouse and a very cheery hen, all in a row.

'We're waiting for a train,' said Ginger.

CHAPTER TEN

Victory

The journey back to the signal box was like a carnival procession. The younger cats were singing, and Old Grey himself invited Mouse to ride on his back, while Jinny rode happily on Robbie's shoulders. They poured into the signal box, and food and drink were quickly prepared.

'Mrs H.,' said Ginger, 'if you had been a dinner-lady, instead of deciding to join the Air Force, the food would be ready.'

'I really must congratulate you, madam,' said Old Grey. 'A brilliant tactical move.'

Mrs Henrietta James fluffed out

her feathers proudly and settled on the table.

'A toast! A toast!' shouted the cats. Robbie stood up.

'I should like to thank you all, on behalf of my friends, for the great service you have done us tonight. We shall never forget your courage and friendship. I propose a toast to our friends the cats!'

The cats cheered themselves heartily. Then Siam jumped on to the table.

'And I propose a toast to the toys. I have seen them in action tonight and I am proud to call myself their friend.'

'What about Ginger?' shouted Stripe. 'Has the cheekiest cat in the country nothing to say?'

'Friends,' said Ginger, rising slowly, 'cats, toys, spiders, beetles, and anyone else who may be listening; I do not speak because I am thinking.'

Loud cheering broke out again.

'I am thinking,' continued Ginger, waving her paw, 'that we do not know how to get back into the house. I have had one or two ideas. Shall we, for example, use the garden seesaw? We could put Robbie on one end, all jump on the other and catapult him through the window.'

'Yes,' shouted all the younger cats.

'No,' shouted Robbie.

'And Jinny,' continued Ginger. 'We could turn the hose on full, lift her up on the jet of water, and shoot her through the window.'

'Yes,' shouted the younger cats.

'Certainly not,' answered Jinny. 'Anyway, the curtains would get soaked.'

'And as for Bear,' decided Ginger, 'we could simply hold his legs, rush at the door, and use him as a battering ram.'

'Yes,' shouted the young cats, who were a bit excited.

'Yes, all right,' agreed Bear. He was sure he was as strong as the door.

'Seriously, though, we do have a problem,' said Robbie, 'and we haven't got long to solve it.'

Old Grey stood up and asked for silence.

'The time has come for our friends to leave us. Black, Siam and Stripe, you will escort them. Show them the shortest route and help them to get into the house.'

They took quite a long time to say goodbye and there were promises to meet again; but at last the toys, with the escort of cats, set off down the old railway line. When they reached the houses the cats knew many short cuts but, even with their help, it was quite light when they got back. The garden gate was open because the milkman had already been.

'This makes it much more difficult,' whispered Robbie, as they crouched in the garage.

And then the back door opened, and they all saw Katy's mother take in the milk.

'That's done it!' breathed Bear. 'They're up.'

'Look here,' said Robbie, 'Bear and

Mrs Henrietta, you are all right. You
were left out last night, so go back to
the garden chairs. Owl, you take
Mouse and go through the window.
Ginger, you can get in that way, too.'

'What about you and Jinny?' asked
Ginger. 'I'll stay with you.' The three
cats were talking together. They
nodded, and Black spoke up:

'We think we can win you enough
time to get in the back door. Get as
near to it as you can, then watch us
carefully.'

Siam ran over to the back door, and Black disappeared round the corner in the direction of the front door.

'Come on,' said Stripe, and he led the others over to the shelter of the water butt.

Siam began to wail. It was a pathetic sound. He sounded like a crying baby. The back door opened and Katy's mother looked out.

'What a beautiful little Siamese,' she said. 'Are you lost?' Siam cried a little more, then rubbed himself against her ankles, making little mewing noises. Then he rolled over on his back and put his paws in the air.

'Oh!' said Katy's mother, quite delighted, 'what a little pet!'

'What a little fibber,' muttered Stripe. 'I've seen them do this double act before. Get ready.'

At that moment, more mewing was heard from the front door.

'Not another one!' exclaimed Katy's mother. 'What on earth is happening?'

She scooped up Siam and went round the corner.

'Now!' hissed Stripe, and Robbie, Ginger and Jinny rushed in the back door. Owl was holding the cupboard door open ready for them and they threw themselves in.

'Ow!' squeaked Mouse, who was just inside the door and was flattened in the rush.

And so, Katy's mother – returning to the back door with Siam in her arms, followed by a black, fluffy cat – found another cat, striped this time, sitting in the middle of the path washing itself. She put Siam down, suddenly less enthusiastic.

'Off you go,' she said, clapping her hands. 'Time to go home. Shoo!'

The three cats turned and gently trotted off down the garden path.

'Quite,' murmured Black. 'It certainly is time to go home. It's been a long night.'

Katy's mother stood watching for several moments, but she did not know what to make of it. Then she caught sight of Bear.

'Oh, that Katy,' she said. 'She's been leaving her toys out again.' She snatched up Bear and Mrs Henrietta James. 'These two need a good wash.'

On her way to the kitchen, she opened the toy cupboard door and found the toys all in a heap.

'These are even worse! What has that child been doing?' She touched Jinny with her finger.

'This looks just like soot, but it can't be. We haven't a fireplace.' She sighed. 'This is a very funny day, and it isn't even breakfast time yet.'

As a result, a beautifully clean group of friends gathered round the kitchen table that evening. Jinny was back in her usual seat. She had insisted on cooking a meal for everyone, and they all sat back feeling full and happy.

'Well, dears,' said Mrs Henrietta James, 'only a short time ago we were sitting here with no idea of the adventures that were going to happen. And here we are again, Jinny safely back, brave little Mouse, and Ginger – where's Ginger?'

Ginger had disappeared. There was a sound, a bit like a rusty trumpet, at the kitchen door, and Ginger stepped in. She was wearing a large towel and a paper crown, and carrying a cushion.

'Don't bother to stand up, my subjects,' she announced. 'The time has come to reward you for your brave deeds.'

She stood in the middle of the room and held the cushion high.

'On this velvet cushion, I have your richly deserved medals. Come forward, Sir Robbie.'

Robbie came and stood in front of Ginger and looked on the cushion. The medals certainly had the Queen's head on them. In fact, they were postage stamps.

'Wherever did you get these stamps from, Ginger?' asked Robbie.

'Nonsense, my child,' said Ginger.

'Can't you see they are royal medals? Sir Robbie, as the starter of the adventure, the seeker of the cats, I award you this medal.'

She licked a stamp and stuck it on Robbie.

'I thank you, Your Majesty,' murmured Robbie, and walked backwards to his seat.

'Owl,' said Ginger, 'come forward, brave bird. As our chief of scouts, I award you the Medal for Good Night Flying.'

'Goodnight, Your Majesty,' giggled Owl.

'And now, brave Bear,' continued Ginger.

The crown slipped a bit, so she hung it on her tail out of the way.

'Bear, I award you the Strength of Ten Medal.'

Bear bowed low and, as a result, got the stamp stuck on the top of his head.

'Mouse,' called Ginger. 'A special award for the courageous Mouse. I give you the Smallest But Bravest Medal.'

Ginger gave the stamp a good lick and stuck it on Mouse's chest.

'Thank you, Ginger,' said Mouse, and he looked very pleased.

'The Lady Henrietta James, please come forward. For outstanding courage in the face of the enemy, the Flying Fishpaste Medal. Oh dear, too much lick,' added Ginger, as the stamp slid off.

'Not to worry, Queen dear,' said Mrs Henrietta, 'I'll stuff it between two feathers.'

'And Jinny,' finished Ginger, 'the Brave Prisoner Medal. Well done, and may you always keep your tail on.'

'Grateful thanks, Oh Ginger Queen,' said Jinny.

'What about you?' asked Robbie.

'To myself,' said Ginger, modestly, 'I award the Order of the Silver Whisker.'

'What's that?'

'It's a medal for cheek,' replied

Ginger. 'Don't you think I've earned it?'

'Of course, Ginger. You most certainly have,' they all agreed.

Ginger draped the towel on her chair and leaped on to it.

'Raise your mugs,' she ordered. 'Three cheers for the heroes – that's us.'

And with the orange juice sloshing a bit in the mugs, the cupboard house rang with three hearty cheers.

THE END

FOG LANE SCHOOL AND THE GREAT RACING CAR DISASTER

BY JOHN CUNLIFFE

'Have you ever seen a picture of a whirlpool? You know how it sucks everything in and swallows it up. Well that's how it was with Don's racing car. It was a classroom whirlpool.'

Class 4 of Fog Lane School is enough to drive any teacher completely round the bend – and it is certainly a big mistake for Sir to encourage Don and his mates in their attempts to build a racing car.

But this is only the start. For the chaos of the racing car ɔject is only the first of Sir's plans to go di. ɔusly wrong and, what with the crazy outing to the Safari Park and the Christmas preparations that get completely out of hand, there is certainly never a dull moment in Class 4. . . .

SBN 0 440 862000

YEARLING BOOKS

A DRAGON IN SPRING-TERM

BY JUNE COUNSEL

'Here we are,' cried Scales cheerfully. 'Spring on Magic Mountain!'

Sam and his friends in Class 4 have a very special friend – a young dragon called Scales. They are all looking forward to seeing him when they go back to school for the Spring term. But Miss Green, their teacher, has put his cave away in the stockroom and firmly tells the class that this term they will be doing new things, starting with a computer. . . .

However, all dragons wake up in the spring, and soon Scales is back with Sam and his friends, leading them all up to Magic Mountain for a series of wonderful adventures!

Scales, the popular young dragon from A DRAGON IN CLASS 4, returns in this amusing and lively fantasy for young readers.

SBN 0 440 862094

YEARLING BOOKS

THE RAFT

BY ALISON MORGAN

'He jumped now, from the dipping bough to the
dipping raft. Instantly it tipped sideways and
slithered out from beneath his feet, towards the
midstream. . .'

Everyone thinks Colin's raft is great – especially
Terry and Ian, Colin's brother. But Terry is
handicapped, with arms only a few inches long,
and Ian can't swim.

Two weeks of rain turn the river into a raging
enemy. Determined to save the raft, Terry and
Ian find themselves in a dangerous struggle
against the terrible power of the river.

An exciting and fast-paced adventure from an
award-winning author.

SBN 0 440 862035

YEARLING BOOKS

If you would like to receive a Newsletter about our new Children's books, just fill in the coupon below with your name and address (or copy it onto a separate piece of paper if you don't want to spoil your book) and send it to:

The Children's Books Editor
Transworld Publishers Ltd.
61–63 Uxbridge Road,
Ealing
London W5 5SA

Please send me a Children's Newsletter:

Name . . . .

Address . . . .

. . . .

. . . .

All Children's Books are available at your bookshop or newsagent, or can be ordered from the following address:
Transworld Publishers Ltd.,
Cash Sales Department,
P.O. Box 11, Falmouth, Cornwall TR10 9EN

Please send a cheque or postal order (no currency) and allow 60p for postage and packing for the first book plus 25p for the second book and 15p for each additional book ordered up to a maximum charge of £1.90 in UK.

B.F.P.O. customers please allow 60p for the first book, 25p for the second book plus 15p per copy for the next 7 books, thereafter 9p per book.

Overseas customers, including Eire, please allow £1.25 for postage and packing for the first book, 75p for the second book, and 28p for each subsequent title ordered.